The Two Sillies

The Two Sillies

Mary Ann Hoberman

ILLUSTRATED BY Lynne Cravath

SCHOLASTIC INC.

New York   Toronto   London   Auckland   Sydney
Mexico City   New Delhi   Hong Kong   Buenos Aires

ISBN 0-439-30505-5

Text copyright © 2000 by Mary Ann Hoberman.
Illustrations copyright © 2000 by Lynne Cravath.
All rights reserved.
Published by Scholastic Inc., 555 Broadway,
New York, NY 10012, by arrangement with Harcourt, Inc.
SCHOLASTIC and associated logos are trademarks
and/or registered trademarks of Scholastic Inc.

12 11 10 9 8 7 6 5 4 3 2 1   2 3 4 5 6 7/0

Printed in the U.S.A.   24

First Scholastic printing, March 2002

The illustrations for this book were done in gouache
with ink on Arches watercolor paper.
The display type was set in Victoria Casual.
The text type was set in Goudy Catalogue.

Designed by Lydia D'moch

For Munro Philip Hoberman,
with love

—M. A. H.

For Beth, Charles, Emma, and Lily

—L. C.

Silly Lilly saw a cat.
Lilly said, "Whose cat is that?"
Sammy said, "That cat is mine."
Lilly said, "I like it fine.
Tell me, please, how can I get
A cat like that to be my pet?"

Sammy said, "Now this is how—
Go cut down those trees right now."
Lilly said, "Now why is that?
Cut down trees to get a cat?"
Sammy said, "That is the way.
You must cut those trees today."

Silly Lilly cut the trees.
Lilly said, "Now, Sammy, please,
Tell me how to get my cat."
Sammy said, "I'll tell you that.
First you have to build a shed.
Go and build it," Sammy said.

"Build a shed to get a cat?"
Lilly asked. "Now why is that?"
Silly Lilly scratched her head.
"That sounds silly," Lilly said.
Sammy said, "That is the way.
Go and build a shed today."

Silly Lilly built a shed.
"Can I have my cat?" she said.
"I've built the shed from all the trees
Can I get my cat now, please?"
Sammy said, "Not yet. Not now.
Now you have to buy a cow."

"Buy a cow to get a cat?"
Lilly asked. "Now why is that?
There's a horse right up ahead.
Can I buy a horse instead?"
Sammy said, "That's not the way.
You must buy a cow today."

Silly Lilly bought a cow.
"Sammy, can I have it now?
I've cut down trees and built a shed
And bought a cow now," Lilly said.
"Take the cow inside the shed
And go and milk it," Sammy said.

"Milk the cow to get a cat?"
Lilly asked, "Now why is that?"
She sat down beside the shed.
"I'm too tired," Lilly said.

Sammy said, "That is the way.
Go and milk the cow today."

Silly Lilly milked the cow.
Soon she heard a low meow.
Lilly wondered, "What is that?"
Then she saw a pretty cat,
Black and white with fur like silk,
Creeping up to sip the milk.

"Sammy! Sammy!" Lilly said.
"Quick! Come here inside the shed!
Look! A cat has come! What fun!
You don't have to get me one.
See, I didn't have to do
All that work you told me to."

Silly Lilly jumped with glee.
Silly Lilly did not see
All the work that she did do
Brought the cat. But Sammy knew.
Sammy smiled and shook his head.
"Silly Lilly!" Sammy said.

Suddenly they heard a squeak.
"Those are mice!" cried Sammy. "Eek!"
Sammy hid behind the cow.
"Take those mice away right now!"

Lilly laughed and shook her head.
"Go and get some hay," she said.

Sammy said, "Go get some hay?
How will that take mice away?"
Lilly said, "I'll show you how.
Go and get some hay right now.
And here is something else to do:
Go and find some catnip, too."

Sammy did what Lilly said.

"Now," said Lilly, "make a bed.
Put the catnip right inside it.

"Cover it with hay to hide it."

Sammy said, "That's very nice.
But how will that get rid of mice?"

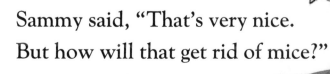

"You will see," said Lilly. "Now
Leave the shed and take the cow."
Sammy led the cow away.
Lilly's cat began to play,
Sniffed the catnip in her bed.
"Shut the door now," Lilly said.

Sammy asked her, "Why is that?
Shut the door and leave the cat?
With no milk for her to drink,
She'll get hungry soon, I think."

Lilly smiled and shook her head.
"Come away now," Lilly said.

Soon they heard a loud meow.
Lilly said, "Let's go back now."
"She is hungry," Sammy said.

But when they found her in her bed,
Sammy said, "Why, look at that!
Your cat has gotten very fat!"

"Look how happy she does seem.
I bet she found a bowl of cream.

"And look, the mice have gone away!
I guess they didn't want to stay.

"You see, I didn't have to do
All those things you told me to."

Sammy laughed and jumped with glee.
Somehow Sammy did not see
How the cat had gotten fed
When he shut her in the shed
With the catnip in her bed.
"Silly Sammy!" Lilly said.

Now Lilly's cat and Sammy's cat
Are full of mice and nice and fat;
And six small kittens roll and play
And take their catnaps in the hay,
While good old cow, inside her stall,
Moos and chews and feeds them all.